The Duke and the Virgin

House of Lords Book 1

1Night Stand series

By
Dominique Eastwick

Copyright © 2016 by Dominique Eastwick
ISBN: 978-1-61333-979-4
Cover art by Cora Graphics

Published by Decadent Publishing Company, LLC
Look for us online at:
www.decadentpublishing.com

Praise for *The Duke and the Virgin*

Oh my!! The Duke and the Virgin is why I love 1Night Stand. When I was done; I smiled with contentment, released a pleased sigh and my heart and soul was filled with warmth. Loved this story!!Got an hour, pick up this book. Your heart will thank you.~ 5 Stars - Got Romance Reviews

This is a great addition to the 1Night Stand series. The Duke is much more likeable than I thought, bored with the same routine, yes, but he's sweet, loves his mother and he is gentle. This is a quick, sexy historical romance. ~ Hearts on Fire Reviews

I don't normally cry when reading erotic romances. This one was so touching, I cried in several places.

What a perfect short read. It delivered more than I expected - good plot, excellent characterization, and amazing sex scenes. ~ Amazon Reviewer

The Duke and the Virgin *was a fast paced romance filled with easy laughter. Witty and sexy, this novel was a blast to read.* ~ Amazon Reviewer

Instant attraction for two hearts who didn't expect much from their encounter; one was bored with life and the other wanted to rid herself of the mystery of what it meant to be a woman. What they found was amazing... Got an hour, pick up this book. Your heart will thank you. ~ Amazon Reviewer

~A Note from the Author~

Dear Reader,

Sometimes writing a short story can be so much harder than a longer one. This was the case with this story. I took on the challenge to see if I could take the 1 Night Stand series to a decade it hadn't gone to yet. I mean it had been everywhere else.

So how to set Madame Eve in a time where woman had so little freedom and show a love story in one night? Now that is a challenge and one I hope I succeeded in pulling off. Judge for yourself!

Happy Reading.

Dom

Dedication

Special thanks to my lovely editors, Val and Kate, who believe in me more than I do. And without them my books would be nowhere.

To the Stephanie Laurens Yahoo Group who for years has supported me, pulled out the large wooden spoon to stir things up, and shared my love of historical romance. I would list you all personally, but this Captain is terrified of forgetting even one of you amazing ladies. Besides, you know who you are :)

To Tracy, Tina, Teresa (the three T's), to Dawn, Tam, Emmeline, Patty, and Dwayne, you are the best friends any one could ask for.

And to Nadine, who is the best beta reader and friend an author could have. I thank you for always being there for me.

Chapter One

"So you are really going through with it?"

Lady Elizabeth Hamilton looked at her lady's maid in the mirror as if she had lost her marbles. "Anna, you told me I should do this."

"Now, *told* might be a bit strong, my lady. I need to be convinced that you have your heart and head set. Because once you do this, there is no going back."

Setting her brush on the dressing table, Elizabeth gave her companion a confident smile, though, to be honest, it was false. "Where is there to go back to? I am not likely to get a proposal this season, any more than I have the seven seasons before. I am helplessly on the shelf. It's not all bad. I get to be myself now. My aunt seems unconcerned that I might live out my life with her in this house."

"We all love you, Miss Llysa, even that father of yours does, in his own way. And I know your aunt would love to have you here for as long as you want.

But—"

Grabbing her hand, Elizabeth silenced her friend. "Anna, I plan to become a woman tonight. Tomorrow, no one will know the difference but me and you. If I am lucky, the evening will be as magical as those novels my aunt hides in the corner of her library. If not, then I'll know that I have at least the knowledge that a woman should have and will be missing nothing by not being wed."

"What about the man? What if he decides to talk?"

"I have to trust Madame Eve. And just in case, I plan to wear this mask." Llysa held the golden mask aloft, twirling it around by its ribbon. "That way he will never know my identity for sure."

Her maid replied with a guarded, "I suppose."

"You hesitate, why?"

"Not many of your class have your figure."

True enough, her voluptuous figure could give her away. She wasn't classically thin with the long neck that the true beauties of the ton possessed. Big bosoms and large hips were her lot in life. Llysa liked

2

her cake and it showed. Food and she were old friends. She had always found happiness in it when she could find it nowhere else. During her first season, she'd nearly starved herself to lose a stone, but it had done little good. Only one marriage proposal from a despot who needed nothing but her money had come her way. Before Llysa could even turn down the proposal, her aunt declared she would disinherit her if her niece considered saying yes. Thank goodness. She had always been her favorite relative.

Now, she led a quiet life, keeping her aunt company, reading more books than she could imagine, and eating the delights the kitchen staff prepared for her. That wasn't to say she did nothing all day. The hours of her days quickly filled between her charitable work, and walks in the park—several a day in fact, even in the rain, with no one around to stop her. She accompanied her aging aunt wherever she wanted to go. But Llysa wanted, nay needed, to know what it would be like to be a woman for one night. Then maybe—she met her reflection in the mirror with a wicked grin—maybe one day she could take a secret lover and he would love her more than the moon.

"You're daydreaming again. I can see it in your eyes," Anna scolded.

"Sorry."

"No need to apologize to me. Your aunt left for the ball fifteen minutes ago. If you are going to sneak out, I suggest you get to it. The rest of the servants are about to sit down for dinner."

"Madame Eve sent a carriage?"

"It's waiting around back. I have the address in case I need to find you. The coachman will wait for one hour after dropping you off in case you change your mind, and will bring you home before sunrise. But he assured me the staff at your destination will be able to find him if at any time you wish to leave."

"Fair enough. And, Anna…thank you."

"Don't thank me yet. You may very well be cursing me for letting you do this, tomorrow." She picked up Llysa's long mantle.

"We will deal with tomorrow when it comes."

4

Anna nodded then peeked out into the hall. Motioning for Llysa to follow her, she made her way wordlessly through the large house. As expected, all the servants were in the dining room in the lower level, none wandering about. They had hours until their mistress would return.

Exiting through the servant's entrance in the back, Llysa embraced Anna before hopping into the unmarked carriage. Only inside did she don her mask and belatedly wonder what she had gotten herself into.

Madame Evangeline, the woman of myth, talked about in hushed whispers, yet no one really knew who she was, and none spoke of her in polite circles. Llysa had first learned of the woman three years earlier, overhearing two women discuss her in the retiring room at a garden party. Anna, ever her champion, had made discreet enquires about Madame Eve at Llysa's request. What began as a way to feed both her and her maid's curiosity eventually turned into a desire to hire the matchmaker's services. On her twenty-fifth birthday, and now firmly nailed to the shelf, Llysa had decided to find out what she offered and how much. Madame guaranteed one night with a man well-suited to her desires, and with complete discretion.

The fee might not be cheap but Llysa had saved her allowance and had nothing better to spend it on. So, when the letter addressed to her, sealed with red wax and embossed with an E, had been delivered, there had been no going back.

As London passed by, she closed her eyes and let the rocking hackney ease her into rest. If the evening went the way she hoped, she would be having a sleepless night.

Chapter Two

His Grace, Wolfe Thane, Duke of Foxhaven and possessing a slew of other titles he cared nothing about, looked up from his book toward the clock on the mantel. *She* would arrive in less than ten minutes. Having arrived himself an hour ago, he'd confirmed everything was in order for their rendezvous. A lifetime of distrust had taught him never to take anything for granted. And since Madame Evangeline seemed to value her anonymity, he knew she would value his. The residence she'd arranged to carry out the date was akin to an upper-class brothel, without the harlots, thankfully. Nestled in an out of the way area of London, it also offered private access. Whoever owned it must be making a pretty penny on dates such as his. Wolfe didn't trust anyone he couldn't look in the eye while speaking, and didn't trust a great many more he could. He needed to ensure he hadn't gotten entangled in a big ruse to get him leg-shackled. As if sensing his concern, the

7

underbutler had shown him a number of escape routes on the way to the room.

"None of the servants will see both of you. Those you see now will be replaced when your date arrives, and then, only the butler will be in contact with you through the night," the young man had informed him.

Ultimately, it didn't matter what happened that night. Wolfe doubted it would be anything but a brief memory by morning. And certainly, with the Season winding down and everyone about to head to their summer homes, it was unlikely he would think on this again. But boredom surrounded him and anything for a bit of excitement seemed like a plan. When he had beat Lord Railey in a game of poker, the despot hadn't a thing to pay his debt with except offer arrangements for a date he had made through Madame Eve. Wolfe had the choice to take the voucher from the man for his date, or wait until the idiot's next allowance came in. Taking said voucher played more to the satisfaction of seeing Railey's disappointment than Wolfe needing a date. But, as the season and its boredoms became more than he could bear, he'd contacted the elusive woman to arrange to replace Railey for the rendezvous.

He was surprised to learn that although he held a voucher, the date could not be transferred from one person to another. If he wanted to use the service, he would have to pay for it. She sent a minion to inform him she had the perfect date if he was interested. Perfect, well, he would see.

What lonely widow, bored wife, or social outcast would walk through the door? Regardless, it would be one night in hundreds that wouldn't have a dull beginning. And that alone improved his outlook.

Sounds of someone arriving downstairs brought him out of his musings. After placing his book on the small spindle table nearby, he stood and listened as he walked to the far corner of the darkened bedchamber. That would give him the advantage when she came in, allowing him a moment to assess her before alerting her to his presence. If the servants were to be believed, only one would speak to her. She would be brought to just outside the room, asked if she required anything, and then left to enter or to leave on her own.

The old door creaked open and soft light from the hall filtered in ahead of the shadowed form of a woman. She stepped in and looked around with an assessing air then, appearing convinced of whatever it was she'd been looking for, she closed the door behind her. Still, he waited until she'd turned her back in the act of removing her mantle and let her guard down. Only then did he step from his hiding place.

"A woman not only on time, but early, is a rare quantity indeed."

Startled, she spun toward him, her face hidden behind a lace demi-mask. Her eyes met his, widened, and, as if by habit, she bowed her head, stopping short of a curtsy. "Your grace."

Tensing, he took another step closer to his mystery lady. "You know me?"

"Of course. Few of the ton, if any, would say they didn't."

To believe his date wouldn't know him had been a fool's dream. Anyone who could afford to be there wasn't likely to be anything but haute ton. "Why the mask, my lady?"

"It would be better, when our paths cross after tonight, that you did not know my true identity."

"But you already know who I am."

She was part of his class, good breeding flowing through every action, from her speech patterns and well-bred accent, to the way she held herself.

"Our situations are completely different, as well you know. Fair or not, women are always judged differently than men."

"So you are assuming our paths will cross."

"I know they will."

He searched her face again, trying to see beyond the mask, looking for something—anything—that would help identify her. "Have I made your acquaintance?"

"We move within some of the same circles in the ton. I would not say we could claim an association, however."

"You intrigue me. So we travel within the same class. You have been to my London house?"

She nodded, although that really didn't narrow down the list. His mother, renowned for her balls, invited nearly everyone. "Have you been to my family estate for our summer party?

"I have not had the pleasure, your grace."

"So not a member of my family's inner circle."

"Certainly not. In fact, I believe, if someone mentioned my name, neither you nor your family would be able to put a face to it."

"Then take off the mask, my lady, as it should matter not if you are a nameless face in the crowd. I promise that, should I see you at a ball, I would do nothing to encourage scandal."

"I cannot." Her uncompromising tone discouraged argument. "If you insist upon seeing my face, then I must leave. "

For some reason, the idea of her leaving disturbed him. Perhaps because, for the first time in recent memory, he was having a conversation with a woman who didn't simper or appear to have designs on his fortune. "Nay, I am only curious, is all. Should you wish to remain anonymous, who am I to complain? I am sure I will forever spend the rest of my days however, looking at women and wondering if one is you." Walking behind her, he allowed his gaze to trail the elegant line of her neck, his dry lips aching to kiss it. He had paid a pretty penny to be there and although she was not a courtesan to be treated as he pleased, he had at least paid for that much.

"May I ask you a question?"

"I am yours to do with as you will, my lady."

"Why would you go to Madame Eve to secure a rendezvous? You're reputation is that of a rogue, your name causing titillation amongst the women of the ton. You could have nearly any of them as a bedmate, so why pay to meet one?"

"Could I have had you? Would you have warmed my bed if I had approached you at a ball?" He knew the answer and it bothered him. She wouldn't have warmed his bed. In fact, she would have likely slapped his face. This a well-bred woman, whose motivations were yet unclear, had turned to Madame Eve for help.

"Actually," he said, "I won the date in a poker game. I contacted Madame Evangeline, who informed me that dates could not be passed to someone else. By then, I was intrigued. To be honest, I am bored, and not even the thought of the Hellfire Club excites me."

He had no idea why he'd needed to tell her any of that. Perhaps he desired to impel her to run. A gentleman never broached the topic of hedonistic clubs created for the sole purpose of allowing high society folks to act out their deepest immoral fantasies. The masked woman put his nerves on end. A strange, new emotion he hadn't experienced or chose to ignore. Ladies in his circle were there to serve him. Starting in the household since his infancy, servants had run at his bidding and later, women served his baser needs.

He frowned. "What about you? Why did you call on the services of the Madame Eve?"

His unnamed lady bit her lip. "I didn't want to go through life a virgin."

Well, that answered the biggest of the questions on his list. "So get married."

"You are under the delusion that women have a say in the matter. If we are not asked, there is very little we can do to rectify the lack. Honorably, that is." She placed her reticule on the chair and started to remove her black gloves. "Being firmly on the shelf, not even on the edge of the shelf, but relegated to the back, I have watched more ladies than I can count enter and exit the marriage mart and I remain, as always, on the sidelines."

Yes, women like her sat on the edge of the dance floor, desperate in their hope that some man, any gentleman, would bless them with his consideration. Pitiful women who, by their very nature of being content with any sort of attention, usually ended with none of it.

"A wallflower."

"You say that like it's a curse. There are worst things than being a wallflower."

"Of course. You could be a wallflower bluestocking."

She shifted abruptly and picked up her discarded pieces, her anger obvious. "I didn't come here to be insulted."

He would not allow this spitfire, bluestocking or otherwise, out the door that evening. Changing tactics, he tugged her close and placed his lips on her bare neck.

Into her ear, he whispered, "No, you came here to be debauched, deflowered, and fucked until you scream. I believe your intent was to find out if the words written in those dirty little novels hidden in every library are true."

She shivered. He must tread slowly. He planned to provoke her within the next minutes. Playing to her curiosity and thirst for sexual knowledge would keep her from running. Trailing a finger along the curve of her jaw, he said, "Tell me what you are feeling."

"Nervous."

"But not scared?"

She shook her head.

"You're trembling." He traced his knuckles across her collarbone. Wrapping an arm around her waist, he brought her against his chest while purposely preventing her from coming in contact with his hardening cock. He opened his hand and placed it over her soft belly. "What are you feeling here?"

She stiffened in his arms, her breathing fast and erratic. "I don't know how to describe it. My stomach is doing circles. Not like when I'm ill, but—I don't know."

Smiling, he slid the hair off her neck and kissed the hollow spot just below her ear. She hissed before leaning into him, doubtless understanding that her body already craved more.

"Here is the game. You answer my questions as honestly as you can, and I will reward you with a new sensation each time."

He couldn't remember when wooing a lady had intrigued him so much. She was a sure thing, after all. He could have her, leave, and never look back. As a well-bred lady who had paid to set up a liaison, she had managed to pique his interest in something other than land, tenants, and laws. The only goal in her mind was to leave the next morning without her virginity. He could take care of that, but something deep within wouldn't allow such callous behavior.

She had a special quality that drew him.

"It's so very strange. Warm and cold all at once."

Lowering the neckline of her dress, he kissed her shoulder. "Where?"

"Between my legs," she whispered.

He hid his surprise with silence. A woman who spoke the truth without being coy? So far he'd struck gold, thanks to Madame Eve. And if the masked lady could afford to pay Madame's high fee, she couldn't come from a family with small pockets. He rewarded her honesty by running his fingers up and over her breasts and feasted his lips on more bare skin. Working to catch her breath, she pushed her marvelous breasts against the bodice of her dress, their heavy weight filling his palms.

"Look at me," he demanded. Without delay or hesitation, she turned to face him, eyes shut. He pressed his mouth to hers, taking advantage of her gasp by delving his tongue past her lips. She gripped his coat and her knees buckled.

Her lids fluttered open, her pale green eyes clear.

"So did the novels do it justice?" He chuckled.

'Not even close, my lord."

"Call me Wolfe, please." He wanted to hear her scream his name in the throes of passion, wanted it imprinted on her that the man, not the duke, had incited that passion in her. He snaked his arm around her waist, pulling her into close contact with his overheated and primed body. His cock strained against the button flap of his breeches. "Do you feel what you do to me? Do you understand?"

She shook her head. "I have no idea."

Grabbing her hand, he encouraged her to work down his chest to his waistband. As if comprehending what he next planned to do, she jerked her fingers away. Her cheeks reddened but before she could avert her eyes from his, he held her chin between gentle, yet firm, fingers. He wouldn't miss her reactions for all the tea in England. Shy eyes met his again. Normally, he'd have described the look as coy, but even having just met her, he sensed no flirtation in her actions. With his cock hard to the point of pain, he stroked her hand over the undeniable bulge.

Eyes wide with shock, she cupped him and

jumped when it twitched in response. Within seconds, however, she grew brave, giggled, and explored more thoroughly. Her lips parted enough to allow the tip of her pink tongue to sneak between them. Images of it licking up his shaft flooded his mind and, for the first time since he'd been an untried youth, a woman threatened to bring him to his knees. After but a few moments in her presence, he sensed his life changing and doubted one night would soothe the ache she'd already created.

He had to gain the upper hand before he lost control. "Are you ready for more?"

Taking a calming breath, she adjusted her gown. "Maybe we could have some tea first?"

"Tea? Perhaps wine would do better." Searching the room for a pull cord, he found none and strode to the door to summon a servant. An open bottle of expensive vintage and stemware sat on a tray on the table in the empty hall. Grateful for the thoughtful staff, he brought the tray in, filled a glass, and handed it to her.

She gulped the wine and handed the glass back

for him to refill.

He stared at it then raised an eyebrow. "You do want to remember this evening, don't you?"

She blushed and glanced away, spotting the book he'd set nearby. *A Journey through India*. Picking it up, she beamed. "Fascinating read. I have always wondered if the descriptions of India are fantasy or factual."

She'd shifted the conversation to something safe and he would give that to her. A few minutes to gain her footing would do them both good. She wouldn't leave anytime soon and they had hours to enjoy each other.

"I suspect the author has never once set foot outside of England."

"Really?" As if the thought that someone could write something they knew nothing about had never occurred to her, she flipped through the pages with interest. Delicate fingers caressed them much like they had his cock only moments earlier. "So you think flying carpets...."

"Are a figment of the author's very active

21

imagination."

"I must admit I considered the same thing." She chuckled and placed the book back on the table.

Closing the distance that separated them, he pulled her into his arms. He didn't want her using that inquisitive brain of hers for conversation any longer, he wanted her to experience. Capturing her lips, he tasted the sweet red wine that lingered, spurring him to deepen the kiss. Though less tentative than the first time, she still hesitated adorably before responding. With the exception of his lips and tongue, he remained still to allow her to explore. He sensed her growing bravery, hoped her graceful fingers would soon caress his body. The longer he spent in her presence, the more he admired her obvious inner strength and ached to know more of her.

Her eyes fluttered open and he didn't want her brain to clear from the fog enveloping her. Not now or ever. Such a thought should have him running from the room, out one of the escape routes the servant had shown him, and back to his safe, if boring, life. Yet his body had no wish to leave. And, he suspected, before morning his very soul would feel the same. He kissed her again, waltzing his tongue with hers, drinking in all she would give him.

His voice hoarse, he said, "Tell me your name."

"Llysa." Gripping his nape, she forced him down for another, deeper kiss.

He cheered silently that she'd given her name, certain it was real, yet just as certain it would not be the one the ton would know her by. Perhaps a pet name her family used. "Llysa," he murmured to taste it on his lips.

Hesitant hands pushed at his lapels, working under his velvet coat, rubbing over the silk shirt. She sighed. "You're chest is so much harder than mine."

"You'll find most of me is harder." Shrugging out of his overcoat, he didn't stop until it landed on the floor, followed by his brocade vest. The best fabrics money could buy lay haphazardly where they fell. He was glad his valet wasn't there.

She stepped back. "I want to see you."

He couldn't help grinning. Llysa wanted to enjoy every part of the evening, not simply lie back and let it happen. With every fiber of his being, he would give her what she desired. After removing his cufflinks and setting them aside, he tugged the shirttails out of his pants, lifted the fine linen over his head then stood before her, naked to the waist. He hoped she found him appealing. He had never cared much if the woman with him thought him attractive. Most were looking for a bedmate, or the draw of money and power, a stronger aphrodisiac than his body. But it mattered a great deal if Llysa liked what she saw.

After what seemed like forever, she reached for him, then stopped, her fingers inches from his skin. It sang with need. She closed the distance and he hissed when her tentative touch on his chest sent tiny sparks straight to his cock. She appeared to enjoy his response and began to explore, but when her palm moved south, he thought he might come. His hand shot up to stop her.

Breathing deeply, he cupped her face. "My turn, minx."

Chapter Three

"Your turn?"

Lyssa had never dreamed she could be so bold. But once his warm skin lay under her daring fingertips, nothing else mattered. Hard muscle jumped at her touch and the triangular patch of hair on his chest fascinated her, not soft as she had expected, but coarse and springy. The tight muscles of his washboard stomach drew her attention, and there he stopped her exploration.

"Don't get scared now." His voice, oh, that voice, did strange and wonderful things to her insides.

"I'm not scared."

"Good, because I want to see what is hiding under all these layers." Warm lips touched the hollow spot under her jaw, distracting her and, until he eased her gown over her shoulder and it fell to the floor, she'd been unaware he'd undone her lacings.

Squeezing her eyes shut, she waited. She stood in front of a man in her undergarments for the first time, and the nerves had begun. Not enough to have her running for the door, but enough to worry he would be less than pleased with what he saw.

"Have you ever seen Russian nesting dolls?"

Thrown by the questions, she opened her eyes. Why would he suddenly speak about a child's toy? "I own a few of them."

"Then you must understand that undressing you is like playing with one of those dolls. I open one to find another beneath it. I took away your gown to find you are still as clothed as you were a moment ago and I wonder how many more layers I will have to work through to get down to you—the doll I'm searching for."

"Two."

He smiled and her stomach did somersaults. "Just two?"

"Well, three, if you count the corset."

"Oh, then we must count the corset as a layer." He spun her and shivers ran the length of her spine as the ties holding her stays relaxed. "What is going on deep within you now?"

"Anxiety."

"Fair enough," he whispered near her ear.

"Giddy."

The corset fell to the floor and he rested his hands on her hips. "And now?"

What did she feel? She shuddered while she considered it. Heat built between her legs as fast as her anxiety. She should leave before the carnal sensations consumed her, but her body wanted, nay, craved more.

"Now I want something, but I am not entirely sure of what that is."

He chuckled. "As it happens, I think I know exactly what that may be."

Seconds later, her petticoat puddled around her slippered feet. Wolfe found the ties holding her bloomers up and she placed her hand over his, stopping him from divesting her of the final barrier to her most private parts. "Wait. I am not ready," she choked. "I don't think I can do this."

"Why do you think you can't?"

Fear engulfed her as all the negative words she

had ever heard about her weight flooded her. Mean words from mean girls. Hurtful words from her uncaring father and siblings. Should Wolfe turn away from her, even masked as she was, she doubted she could show her face in public again. It would be the final blow to her fragile ego. "What if once I am naked you don't want what you see?"

He laid his palms on her shoulders. "Trust me, Llysa."

"I do." She looked at him over her shoulder, heat spreading over her cheeks. "I mean, I want to."

"I can't help you with your virginity if you keep these on."

Clutching at straws, she asked, "Can we blow out the candles?"

"If that's what you really want. But I would prefer to see you in the light. If you are only going to allow me this one night, I want to get my fill of you with all of my senses." Turning her again, he kissed her until she relaxed. With her knees threatening to buckle, she had no choice but to reach up and wind her arms around his neck.

She suspected he knew exactly what he was doing, soothing her into a relaxed state, which allowed him the freedom to untie her bloomers without her protest. The fabric fell, joining the petticoat around her ankles. As cold air hit the back of her legs, she fully comprehended that, with the exception of her chemise, stockings and shoes, she stood bare.

"Lift your arms." His voice, deep and soft, fluttered through her like a warm summer breeze.

I can do this. She had come there for one purpose and had known getting naked would be a part of it. But knowing and doing were two different things. Hesitant at first, she lifted her arms to just above her head. She needed to stop being silly and get on with it. More determined then, she raised them fully. Closing her eyes, she waited until the soft, silky chemise lifted over her head. Only then did she open her eyes and lower her hands, placing them on her full hips. It took every bit of self control not to cover her bare body.

"You are gorgeous." His voice held so much

awe, it forced her to look at him. "Now that I have seen you, I want to taste you."

He walked her backward until the edge of the bed hit the back of her thighs and he gripped her waist, helping her up onto the high mattress. Nudging her legs apart, he said, "This bed is the perfect height."

"Perfect?" she murmured as he stood between her thighs.

"Yes, perfect. Perfect to enter you with. If you were more experienced, I would show you how much, with you at the right height, your legs spread wide." He ran his fingers up and down the inside of her thighs, finally stopping on the pink ribbons holding up her stockings. Slowly he untied them, rolling down one stocking and then the other. "What I wouldn't give to have a thousand nights to show you everything I would like to do to your delicious body."

Forcing down the almost overwhelming desire to tell him she wanted that, too, she threw back her head and focused on the wanton sensations he created when he bent over her and savored the skin at her neck. Focusing on them prevented her from dwelling on the fact that at the end of the night there could be no future between them. The most she could hope for was a position as his mistress. She would rather be alone and celibate than spend the rest of her days wanted only for her abilities in bed. Without a doubt, he could teach her everything she needed to know, but what would those lessons do to her?

"Stop thinking," he grumbled, kissing his way across her collarbone. "Every time you do, you tense."

"Sorry."

He raised his head and locked his sparkling blue eyes on hers. "Just don't think."

"I always think." She sniffed.

"I feared you would say that."

"Excuse me?"

He gave her a smug grin. "I am going to have to ensure you are so senseless with lust you will only think of me making love to you all night long."

"All night?"

"Oh, yes"

She gulped. "Is that even possible?

"In so many different ways." Punctuating each word with a kiss, he moved lower until level with her taut nipple. When he took it into his mouth, all thought of words or even how to form them disappeared. Chills that had nothing to do with the cool air shot down her spine. No wonder so many women talked about getting His Grace, Wolfe Thane, into their bedchamber. She suspected not as many were visited by him as claimed. If so, then the man never slept. But who needed sleep when she could do something as amazing as this?

"I adore the little noises you make," he said against the underside of her breast.

Boldly, she ran her fingers through his hair and admitted, "I adore how you help create them."

"Just wait." Never taking his eyes off hers he eased down her body, forcing her legs farther apart. Kneeling, he gave her another devilish smile before lifting each of her legs over his shoulders. "Listen carefully, Llysa. Do. Not. Think."

He commanded the way he'd been born to do and she knew she would follow him wherever he commanded. Yet as his mouth brushed her inner thighs, she hesitated, not because she thought about not thinking, but because she had never imagined any man putting his lips there. He nibbled, a slight bite, but enough to tell her not to think.

As she worked hard to obey his order, his tongue touched her in the one place she had read about but hadn't believed actually happened. Wolfe licked the most private part of her body. With one stroke of his tongue across skin she never dared to touch except when necessary, small explosions burst through her. Her fingers tightened in his hair and she arched. If enjoying this made her wanton, she wanted to be wanton.

He circled her sensitive flesh and when she couldn't possibly bear any more, he sucked. Shaking with unexplainable need and desire, she nevertheless couldn't imagine there could be more than this. His hands rested on her hips and tugged her closer. Without warning, every muscle in her body tightened and, from the pit of her stomach, a detonation rocketed through her. Her world fractured and she screamed, fear mixing with insane desire, and he never ceased his ministrations until the last shiver rocked her body.

Standing, he took her into his arms, allowing her to recover. She opened her eyes slowly, for surely the world would look different. On fire, perhaps. Because she had been raised to believe pleasure like that would send her straight to the depths of Hell. But the room appeared the same. Hunger still burned in Wolfe's eyes. The only change that had occurred had been within her.

"Are you all right?" The concern in his voice broke down the last wall around her heart. So determined had she been to keep her emotions out of the evening, yet how had she believed that possible? She'd experienced more in the last five minutes than she had in her entire life.

Nodding, she bit her lip. "Was that...?"

"An orgasm? Yes, and one of the most beautiful I have ever seen or tasted. And now that you know a woman's pleasure, I can't wait to help you become a woman in every other sense." He arched a brow.

"Tell me, have you ever seen a man naked?"

She swallowed hard. "Only in art at the museum, and then only when I could sneak a peek."

"Well, that is something, at least." His fingers paused at his waistband. "Do you want to undress me or watch?"

"I'm not sure I can move my muscles yet."

Leaning in, he claimed her lips. "You are so good for my ego." His body reminded her of the replica she'd seen of Michelangelo's *David*. She wanted to touch him, wanted to feel his warmth.

Standing between her parted legs again, he placed her hands on his bare chest. In awe, she roamed her palms over the hard muscles. So in awe, in fact, she wasn't aware he had kicked his pants off until he led her curious fingers to his erect manhood, holding her against him.

Hesitant, she began to pull away, but he tightened his hold, insisting her hand remain. As her nervousness eased, curiosity roared to the surface. She wrapped her hand around him and he hissed. Startled and afraid she'd hurt him, she began to retreat again, but he shook his head then taught her the stroking rhythm he enjoyed until she did it willingly and without fear.

He groaned. "That's it."

Staring at his remarkable girth, she asked, "How is that going to fit inside of me?"

"I will fit, but we will take it slow. Your body is created to take my cock." He eased her back on the bed until they lay side by side. "Do you trust me?"

"Yes."

"Then, please, will you get rid of the mask so I may see the whole of you?"

For a brief second, she hesitated. She wanted to take it off. Closing her eyes, she tried to remember the reasons she wore the disguise. In the morning, she would be no more than an addition to the number of women whose beds he had graced. As much as she would have liked to believe differently, the only option for her to continue with him after this evening would be to become his mistress, and only if he asked. No. Better to be in the same room and never have him know they had shared an evening together.

Shaking her head, she prepared to roll away.

"Be still." His fingers brushed the soft lace of her mask. "Although I would love to see the face of the woman I am making love to, I will respect your desire."

"I'm sorry I just...."

"Shhh. I don't want any regrets tonight." His lips captured hers, silencing anything else she might have said.

Disappointment wracked Wolfe, which, like his nervousness earlier, wasn't a familiar emotion for him. In fact, he couldn't remember the last time he'd been truly disappointed in something. Of course, there were things he wished were better or different, but true disappointment was something else entirely. Not showing him her face told him she didn't want more with him after their one evening together. And he already knew he wanted to know Llysa much longer than a few hours.

When she sat on the edge of the bed, it would be so easy to open the buttons of his breeches and release his cock from its confines. Sheathing himself deep within her would be exquisite, but her virgin body would be unable to take him, much less enjoy him at that angle. And he wanted her to enjoy every second of what he planned.

And afterward, after their liaison had ended, he wanted her to desire him from across the room at every ball. To want him so much she would cross the dance floor and tell him so. Drawing back in shock at the realization of how far under his skin she'd gotten, he shook his head.

"What's wrong?" Confusion filled her eyes— green eyes he could spend hours staring into.

He smiled. "Nothing, my lady." When he put his mind to something, he could do anything, and if he wanted her crossing a crowded ballroom to get to him at a later date, he must do everything in his power now to compel her to do so. She would forget everything ever taught her about the ton, about the rules and proprieties of society.

Rolling over her, he held himself up enough that he didn't cover her. She must understand his power, and desire more of it. He loved the way her breath caught in surprise and her hands hesitated, unsure where she should place them. Trailing kisses over her neck, he tasted every inch she allotted him. Feathery brushes of his fingers began at her shoulder and downward, giving her only enough to entice but never enough to soothe. She needed to burn for him.

When his hand finally finished its journey down her breasts, over her full hips, and to the apex of her thighs, he found her wet and ready. He dipped one finger inside and she was as tight as he expected. Her inner walls clenched around him and he nearly came. Every ounce of willpower he'd spent his adult life cultivating prevented him from taking her.

"Breathe, Llysa."

"Trying to." She whimpered, shifting against his hand.

"Do you think you can you take more?"

Popping her head off the pillow, she squeaked, "More?"

Chuckling, he couldn't remember the last time he'd enjoyed foreplay as much. He rubbed her clit and when her head fell back, he eased a second finger inside. Working her into another impassioned frenzy, he prepared for the right moment to take her. The telltale signs of her shallow breathing, her death grip on his arms, and her body working his fingers told him she was nearly there. "That's it, Llysa."

She flew over the edge, her head thrown back in pleasure, mouth open, and the sexiest moan he'd heard passed her lips. Her thighs slammed shut around his arm as the orgasm raked her body. He didn't ease up until he'd dragged every shudder and moan from her he could. When her legs relaxed, he positioned himself over her, nudging them apart again. As she stared up at him, her eyes heavy-lidded and still cloudy with pleasure, he entered her in one quick thrust and breached her maidenhead easily, but she tensed and her expression changed from pleasure to pain.

A single tear slipped under her mask. He hated himself for causing her discomfort. With the pad of his thumb, he wiped the tear away and, hoping to ease her, whispered, "Relax, my darling. That's the worst of it."

She nodded wordlessly. Though impatient, he waited, when the primitive male part of him urged him on. Still, he waited. For the first time in his life he, cared about something other than his own pleasure and he refused to rush.

Locking her eyes with his, she swallowed hard then tilted her hips, as if curious.

"That's it," he encouraged, gritting his teeth. And still he waited.

He let her lead the dance. Only when she was ready would he take over. Not knowing a lot about virgins, Llysa being the first he had slept with, he understood she needed time to stretch, to get used to having him inside her. Only then could he take over again.

"You seem in pain," she managed between breaths.

"Blissfully."

"I don't understand. Tell me."

She wanted him to talk to her? He only wanted to heed the devil within that said to take his pleasure.

"Holding back to give you time to…adjust is taking a great deal more self-control than I had anticipated."

"Does it help if I do this?" Lifting her hips, she forced him deeper.

"Fuck me." He groaned again and the chit had the audacity to giggle. He was dying and she was laughing. Any woman who'd just had her maidenhead breached and could giggle couldn't be as fragile as he thought her to be, thank God. "You are a minx."

Claiming her mouth, he took her laughter into his. Then he gripped her full hips, and drove his cock into her. Her mirth turned to gasps, but she met each thrust. Her small hands inched from his shoulders down to his bare ass, nails scoring the skin in their path, pushing him on until he heard nothing but a roaring thunder in his ears.

As if by instinct, she wrapped her legs around his waist, allowing him deeper access and sending him to heaven's gate. Holding off, he spurred her on, kissing her damp neck until she shivered. When her thighs clamped around him and the first screams of pleasure left her luscious lips, he fell over the cliff to orgasmic bliss. And for a time thought of nothing except the beautiful woman under him.

After her breathing slowed, she whispered, almost to herself, "Why would anyone think of England at a time like this?"

Propping up on his elbows, he laughed. "What are you talking about?"

"Well, my mother told my sister the night before she wed that she should lie back and think of England on her wedding night."

"Really? And how, might I ask," he rolled to his side and slid his fingers across her cooling body, "would you know this?"

She blushed all the way to her beautiful, pert nipples. "I might have been eavesdropping."

"Of course you were." He tugged her close, wanted her against him. It occurred to him she might require more care than the ladies who had shared his bed in the past, none of whom he managed to picture in his head. Only this woman mattered. Lifting all the way up, he groaned. "Stay there."

"Where would I go? My muscles no longer seem

to work."

He grinned. *Not a bad thing.*

A large basin of water sat in the corner with some fresh cloths. Bringing them to her, he washed away the remnants of her virginity from her thighs. "How does a bath sound?"

"Heavenly."

Wolfe crossed the room, stopping to throw on the robe warming on a chair near the fireplace. Opening the door, he wasn't surprised to see the butler standing outside.

Before Wolfe could ask, the man said, "A bath has been prepared in the adjoining room, your grace."

"Thank you."

With a bow, the elderly servant took a step back against the wall. "My pleasure."

Walking into the room connected to the bedroom, Wolfe found the steaming bath ready. He returned to their bed and scooped Lyssa into his arms.

"Stop! I am too heavy."

"Says who?"

"Everyone says I am a stone or two overweight."

"Everyone is a fool. You are perfect." He meant every word. This woman might be perfect—for him. Entering the bathroom, he eased her into the water. "How are you feeling?"

She slipped down into the water with a sigh. "Wonderful and sore all at once."

"Lean forward." When she did without question, Wolfe smiled and slid down behind her.

"Do you always share a bath after—you know...."

Even with her back to him, he spotted the rosy blush on the tips of her ears. "After making love? No, this is the first time I have shared a bath with anyone." He took the cloth and soap sitting on the stool next to the tub and rubbed it over her back.

"I don't understand."

"I don't completely understand either," he admitted, rinsing the soap from her shoulders.

She played with the suds on the water's surface. "You aren't the man the ton thinks you are."

"No one is really who the ton thinks they are. For example, they think you are just a wallflower, yet you have an inner sensuality that brings me to my knees. And you are so much stronger than I think even you know."

"I am not strong." She shook her head and touched her mask as if to ensure it hadn't shifted.

"Aren't you? You came here and quickly put me in my place, standing your ground when I was purposefully hurtful, intentionally rude. You met me thrust for thrust in bed, didn't hesitate—oh, I do love this blush of yours." He traced the shell of her ear with his finger, avoiding the ties of the mask.

"I hate to contradict you, your grace, but I am a coward. I can't even bring myself to take off this mask although you have seen every other inch of me."

He brushed his lips over her shoulder. "I have thoroughly enjoyed every inch I have seen and tasted."

Several moments passed before she finally spoke again. "I am afraid of almost everything. I am afraid of my father, of growing old and being a burden to my family, and I am sad that I'm so afraid to remove my disguise that you will see me at a ball and not know who I am."

"Let me see you."

"I can't because I am as equally afraid that you will see me at a ball and know who I am." She wrapped her arms around her knees and rested her chin on them. "I know that makes no sense. "

"Lyssa, you don't need to explain to me." He stood and snatched a towel off the stool. "Come, the water is cooling. Let's get you back to bed."

"You're coming with me?"

He hated the uncertainty in her voice and common sense advised him to tuck her in and run, hard and fast. But his heart, whose sole purpose up until that night had been merely to pump blood, told him if he only had a few hours, then to take what he could. If he married, and God knew he would have to one day, he wanted this night to remember. "I wouldn't miss it for the world."

It did not surprise him to find the bedroom cleaned, linens changed, and bed covers pulled down. Their clothes had been folded neatly on a chair and a tray of food waited for them. The staff was nothing if not efficient and silent in their tasks.

After bringing the tray to the bed, he discovered great joy in feeding her and being fed in return. For a woman who had been a virgin not more than an hour earlier, Llysa seemed very comfortable, by no means a wilting maid. She sat cross-legged on the bed wearing nothing but her mask, and he found her openness refreshing.

Having finished her second glass of wine, she asked, "So are we going to…make love again?"

Shaking his head, he said, "As detectible as your body is, and as you can see I am ready to go again, you need time to heal. I can't in good faith take you again and look at myself in the mirror in the morning."

"Some rake you are."

"Don't tell anyone, but I never really was."

"And yet you talked tonight about being a member of the Hellfire Club."

"I lied." He nearly choked on a piece of cheese at the look of surprise on her face.

"You lied? But you're a duke."

"Even dukes lie on occasion. I said it to scare you. I was curious if you would run. You see, I didn't lie when I said I was bored, and at times I admit to playing games." Her clear eyes held a mixture of worry and hurt. He cringed knowing his selfish actions caused such pain. "I am not playing with you now."

She took another bite and nodded, but refused to meet his eyes again. While so strong on the outside, she had a delicate nature that his heart ached for. She had to be strong to live the life she did. People believed she didn't care what they thought. As an on-the-shelf wallflower, she had learned to portray a façade to the world that she didn't care if she married or not, and had more important things to do. For the first time, he considered the unfairness of her situation.

Pushing the food out of the way, he inched closer to her and tipped her chin back. "Lyssa, look at me." He waited for her to meet his gaze. "I will never play with your emotions again. This I promise."

He captured her mouth, demanding she open and acknowledge his remorse and the truth of his words. She didn't fight him and when his other hand cupped her bare breast, she sighed and met his kiss with a fevered one of her own.

"I'm sorry if I hurt you," he murmured against her lips.

"I'm being silly—too sensitive."

"You make me want things I have never wanted." Shifting so his back rested against the stack of pillows in front of the headrest, Wolfe drew Lyssa into his arms and, without questioning, she snuggled against his chest. "I want to protect you. I have grown up knowing I should take care of women. Yet I know you can take care of yourself, I want to care for you."

"I wish life were different," she said then silence filled the room.

What more could he say? He rubbed her back and ran fingers through her hair, careful not to dislodge the mask, until her breathing slowed and she slept peacefully in his arms.

The few hours left of the evening flew by too

quickly and when the scratch on the door came to alert Wolfe that their time together neared an end, he faced it as he did all issues—head on. Carefully easing Llysa to the side, he noticed her mask had slipped. But as much as he wanted to know her face, he wanted her trust more. Without looking at her, he readjusted the lace then slid out of bed.

Once he'd dressed, he laid a kiss on her exposed cheek. "Sweeting, it's time to leave. Your carriage is waiting."

Her eyes fluttered open and she smiled up at him before her hands flew up to check her mask. "Thank you for not removing it," she whispered.

"I thought about it." He strode over to stoke the fire. "Come, you don't have a lot of time, you must be home soon. Your servants will be up within the hour."

After helping her dress, he walked her as far as the bedroom door. This had been their domain and she'd been clear that after tonight she couldn't have him in her life. But he planned or hoped some distance would change her mind.

He pulled a card from his breeches pocket then reached over to the side table and picked up the cuff links he had set there. "Should you ever need me, show these to my butler, and he will admit you. I will come immediately."

She shook her head. "I can't take these." Were those tears in her eyes? The damnable mask prevented him from being sure.

"Please...I will feel better knowing you have a way to get through my protective staff. My card and these will do it. I took care, but there could still be repercussions of our night."

"You mean a child?"

"Yes."

Her hand glided to her stomach and a part of him wished he had not pulled out before his orgasm. But he wouldn't trap her any more than she would trap him. He folded her fingers around the card and cufflinks in her palm and then bent to brush his lips over hers. "I will always come to your aid."

"Thank you for a magical evening," she said.

"It was, as you already know, my pleasure, my

lady."

Walking through the doorway, she turned, curtsied, and lowered her head. "Your grace." And disappeared down the hall, leaving him hard-pressed not to follow.

Chapter Four

Three weeks later

"His grace, your grace," His mother's butler announced as Wolfe walked into her morning room, although it happened to be three in the afternoon.

"Mother." He kissed her proffered cheek.

"What brings my favorite son here on such a miserable day?" She swept a hand toward the rain steadily tapping against the window.

Sitting in the seat across from her, he waited while she ordered some food and tea. "First, I am your only son and, second, do I need a reason to visit my mother?"

"I know you better than that. The House is in its last week in session and you take time to leave your seat to see me. What is it?"

"Really, Mother," he replied. "You are entirely too skeptical."

"Like mother, like son."

He cleared his throat. "I do have a favor to ask."

Her shrewd eyes met his. "I am all ears, my dear."

"I need you to host a ball."

If her eyebrows shot any higher they would have disappeared into her hairline. "A ball, you say? Do you plan to attend?"

"Well, it would be silly to ask you to host it at my request and not show up myself."

"Who do you want me to invite and when do you want this to happen?"

He grinned. His mother could never resist the opportunity to host a ball. "The ton. And this weekend."

His mother jumped to her feet. "Everyone? This weekend? As in five days?"

"Meaning every member of the ton, in five days." His smile widened.

"I suppose you have a theme in mind as well?" She sank onto the cushions again.

"Masquerade."

"Wolfe, have you lost your mind? What is going

on? Are you planning to steal the Crown Jewels or something?"

Drama, thy name is Mother. "No, I am not planning to do anything of the sort. Can you host it?"

"Of course I can." She harrumphed as if insulted he would think she couldn't pull off the impossible. "So, tell me…who is she?"

Not bothering to deny her suspicions, he said, "I don't know her name. Her real name, that is. How did you know?"

"The most eligible duke of the season, or the last five seasons, for that matter, shows his face at more balls and events in the last two weeks than he ever has. Believe me when I tell you, people are talking." A maid carrying a tray of food stood in the doorway and his mother rose and slammed the door in her face. "What do you mean, you don't know her name?"

"I met her a few weeks ago, but she wore a mask."

"Curious." His mother tapped her chin. "Are you sure she will come to this ball?"

"I am banking on her not being able to resist."

"And if you find her, what are your plans?"

"I plan to make her my duchess and live happily ever after."

His mother's smile lit the room, "Now that is an idea I can't resist. Go help that poor girl in the hall with the food tray then ring for my secretary. And I suggest you send all of your servants over here to help. This is going to take a miracle to accomplish."

***

Lyssa looked around the ballroom as best she could. Wolfe stood a good head taller than most and she hoped that height would make it easier to find him. She didn't believe one more person could inch their way in. The guests overflowed into the side rooms, and the crowd had begun to spill into the well-lit gardens. To call the party a crush would be an understatement. Still, she wondered why she'd had the nerve to come. But deep inside, she knew. She needed answers to the questions in her head. She wanted, had to know, if Wolfe would recognize her.

Would he look for her and what would he do if he found her? The biggest question: how far would she go to be with him again?

She had hidden at her sister's estate outside of London for the first couple of weeks after the night she'd spent with Wolfe. But one could only stay and listen to how much of a burden one was before leaving. And a fortnight had been long enough. Her aunt didn't say *I told you so*, but only just. The inclement weather had been good enough reason not to go about town, but that wouldn't last. When the invitation for the masquerade ball arrived and her aunt announced *we aren't missing this for the world*, Lyssa didn't argue.

So there she stood, on the edge of the dance floor, hoping to catch a glimpse of her duke, while wondering how her aunt would deal with Llysa's decision to become his mistress. If he accepted her offer. She knew how the rest of the family would react, but as they treated her like an outcast anyway, she didn't care. But she did care what her aunt thought. Fingering the cuff link she'd had designed into a necklace, Llysa prayed it would give her the strength to follow her heart.

Ten minutes turned to twenty, twenty turned to an hour, and she began to think maybe she wouldn't see him. As another minute then another ticked by and each strain of music played, her confidence waned. No one had invited her to dance, not that she'd expected anyone to but once again, she knew she didn't belong. Even when she wore a mask, no one wanted to know her.

Backing into the crowd to find her rightful place along the fringes of society, she froze when two strong hands gripped her waist. Hope swirled with fear. She waited, the strong grasp preventing her from turning.

"Tell me you don't love me and I will leave, never bothering you again." Warm breath near her ear caused shivers to skate down her spine.

She shook her head and, when he loosened his hands, turned to find him closer than she'd expected. Meeting the beautiful blue eyes she would know anywhere, she said, "I can't say that."

"Thank God." Wolfe huffed and took her hand, tugging her through the crowd until he found an empty room. He snatched away the demi-mask he wore and claimed her lips. Her knees threatened to give out, but his strong arms kept her upright. "I have missed you."

"I've missed you, too." She breathed in the rich smell of brandy and the crisp starch scent of his shirt.

"Where have you been? I have attended every ball held over the last three weeks."

Looking up at him, she couldn't hide her shock. "Really? You never go to balls except those held by your family."

"Exactly."

"I went out of town at first."

His fingers traced her cheekbones. "That explains it."

She fiddled behind her neck until the necklace came off. Placing it in his hand, she said, "You said if I needed anything."

"Anything."

"I need you. I want to be yours."

"How do you want me?"

She dropped her chin and inhaled deeply. "Any way you will have me. I'll be your mistress if that is the only thing I can be. I love you, Wolfe, and I die inside at the thought of being without you."

"Shhh." He placed a finger against her lips. "I have no need for a mistress, Lyssa."

"Oh. I just thought…." Embarrassment filled her and, leaping out of his embrace, she headed for the doorway.

"Lyssa, wait." He gripped her elbow but she jerked away.

"I read too much into this. I'm a fool."

"Lyssa, I don't want you as my mistress. I want you as my duchess."

She stilled, certain she had heard him wrong. "You can't."

"I assure you, I can." He got down on one knee. "I love you."

"But you have never seen my face nor have I told you my real name." She sank to the floor with him. "You don't know me."

61

"But I do. We talked more during that one night than I have with any woman my entire life." He kissed her again.

She paused. "My father is Viscount Rutherford."

"I have met your father." Wolfe barely held back a sneer, but his eyes held disdain.

"Exactly. He isn't anyone's favorite man, and I am his daughter." Surely Wolfe wouldn't want her as his duchess now.

"Who your father is doesn't change the way I feel about you." His thumbs rubbed the edge of her mask just above her cheekbone. "Who are *you*, Llysa?"

"Elizabeth Hamilton. I live with my aunt, Lady Clarissa Trombly."

"Lyssa. That's what your aunt calls you?"

"Yes." Lifting her face, she waited for him to reach behind her head and remove the mask. Yet even after asking her to marry him, he waited for her permission, respecting her privacy. That alone would have been enough to ensure she loved him. At her nod, he tugged at the ties and she closed her eyes as the soft lace mask fell away. He said nothing for so long she feared he had left her. Opening her eyes again, she found him staring back with such love and adoration she nearly cried.

"I know you. I have always thought you were beautiful. I know you don't believe me, but I remember you wore the richest green velvet to my uncle's holiday ball last year. You talked with no one all night but read your book in the corner, only leaving to get your aunt something to drink."

"You remember me?" How could that be?

"I remember you. Marry me, Llysa."

Love bloomed in her chest. "Yes."

Hauling her into his arms, he kissed her hair. "Thank God."

The door swung open and his mother stormed in, with Lady Trombly and the servant whom Wolfe had positioned at the door to assure their privacy, following on her heels.

"Well, she seems to be thoroughly compromised," his mother announced with no small degree of satisfaction.

Wolfe sighed and came to his feet, bringing Llysa with him. "Mother, she said yes."

"Of course she did, but we wanted to be sure. Welcome to the family, Llysa." Walking back to the entrance, his mother smiled. "You chose well, too, Wolfe. When I saw you leaving with Lyssa in tow, I had to be assured she join us. So many chits these days haven't a brain to call their own. I am impressed, Wolfe. I underestimated your ability to find the perfect wife."

Tearing happily, Lady Trombly first embraced Llysa then followed Wolfe's mother out of the room. The two began discussing wedding plans before the door had shut behind them.

"Shall we announce our engagement?" Wolfe asked when the room had cleared.

Still unable to comprehend it all, Lyssa nodded, afraid if she spoke, the bubble of happiness would somehow burst. But as her husband-to-be wrapped an arm around her, infusing her with strength and love, she knew this would be forever.

"Are you by chance with child?" he asked.

64

Looking into his clear eyes, she shook her head. "Well, that is something we will remedy on our wedding night."

With their fingers intertwined, she let him lead her out into the ballroom. And though she might have been a wallflower, no one in the ton could deny she was now *his* flower. He declared his affection to her in full view of the ton. If she hadn't been compromised when her aunt and his mother walked in on them, she was after the kiss had the entire ton declaring they had never seen such a love match before.

When the excitement died down and everyone who had ignored her in the past had congratulated her, Wolfe dragged her away, up a hidden staircase and into a large masculine bedroom. Pulling her into his arms, he whispered against her neck, in the spot he knew would drive her crazy with lust, "I thought we could practice for our wedding night."

Lyssa thought, as he led her to the bed, that was a mighty fine idea indeed.

About the Author

Award-winning author Dominique Eastwick grew up a US Navy Brat, so if there was a naval base, that was probably home. She currently resides in North Carolina with her husband, two children, crazy lab and lazy cat.

Dominique's love of reading started when she was told to read *To Kill a Mockingbird* in high school—a book that opened her eyes to the joys of reading and entering into the world of the author. To this day she ranks this book as her favorite.

Also by Dominique Eastwick

Strawberry Kisses

The Marquis and the Mistress

The Earl and His Virgin Countess

Shifting Hearts

Healing His Soul's Mate

Infiltrating Her Pack